The Magic Christmas Star

Forever Friends™

It was
Christmas Eve,
and the moon was bright.
Robin's eyes shone —
how excited he was!
Christmas Day was near...

But hush – what was crunching
through the deep snow?
Could it be somebody's footsteps?

Robin followed the sound
and it led to
a magical sight!

Santa looked worried, he stopped suddenly.

His lantern swung this way, then that.

'Oh dear', he sighed. 'Which way should I go?'

Robin flew down to help.

Together they walked leaving
tracks in the snow — footprints
so huge and so tiny.
At last, Robin stopped near
a cottage in the wood — the home
of his friend, Little Bear.

But now poor Santa looked
more worried than before —
he'd forgotten Little Bear's
Christmas present!

Bear Cottage was wrapped in a blanket of snow.

Inside, paws were busy and faces were bright —

getting everything ready for Santa...

Santa's delicious Christmas Eve treats were left for him under the tree!

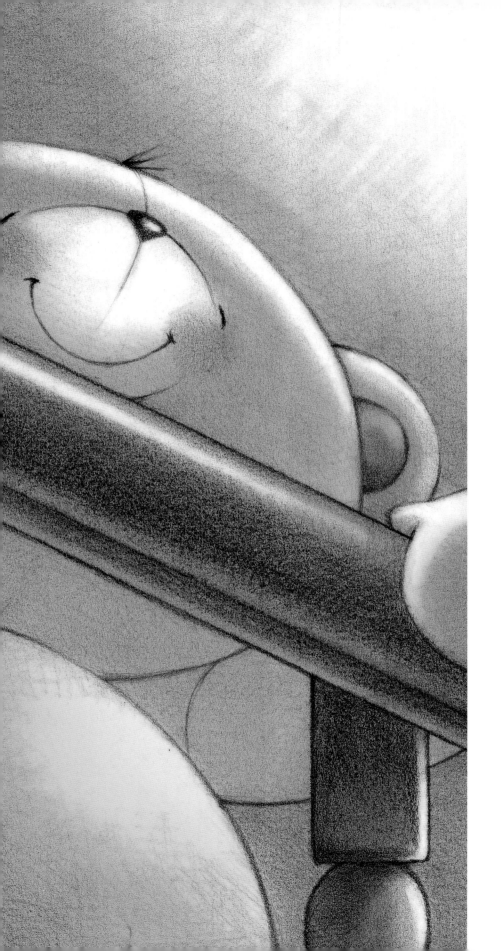

Little Bear peeped down
from the stairs, giggling excitedly.
Christmas Day was just
one dream away – nothing
could be more special!

It was way past Little Bear's bedtime
but there was *one* last job to do.

Three Christmas stockings were
carefully hung by the fire,
before the bears yawned
and went up to bed...

...no peeking!

Little Bear's bedroom sparkled as moonbeams streamed in through the window. Tonight was the night when wishes came true! So Little Bear blew a wish to the moon for a glimpse of something magical.

But the only magical something out there was now peeping in from the snow.

It was chirpy and fluffy and a wonderful friend...

...and had come to say goodnight!

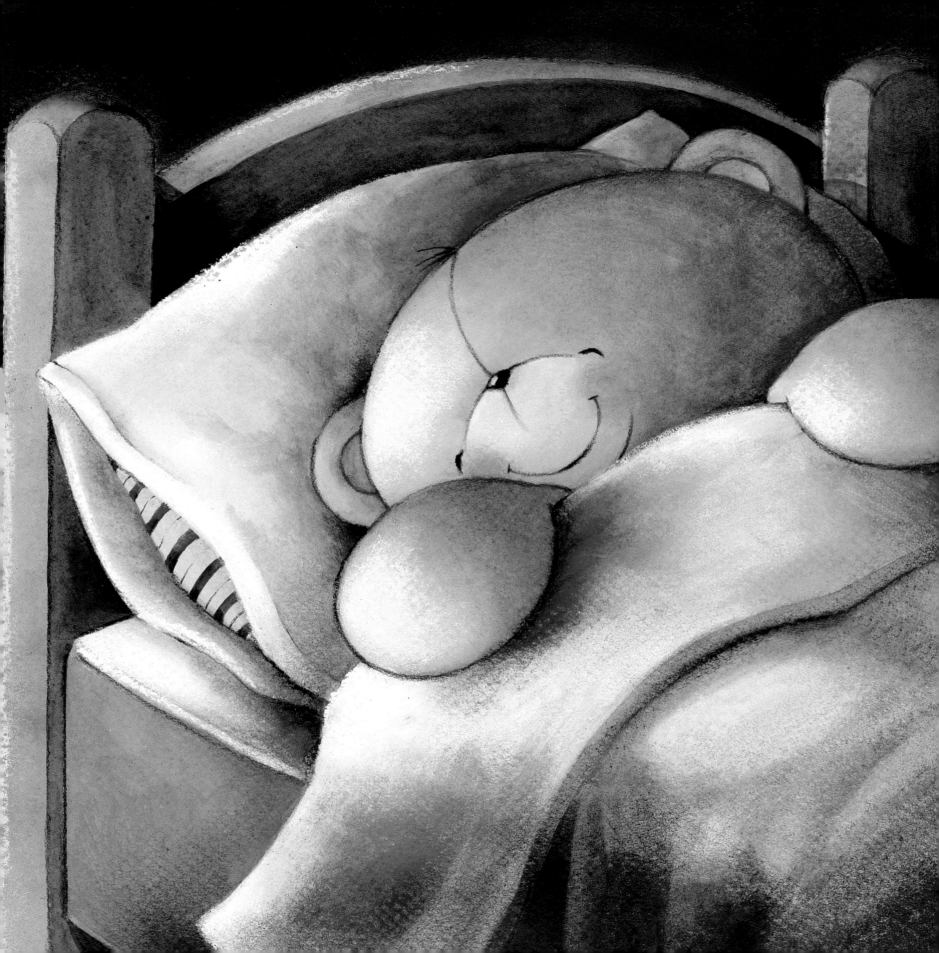

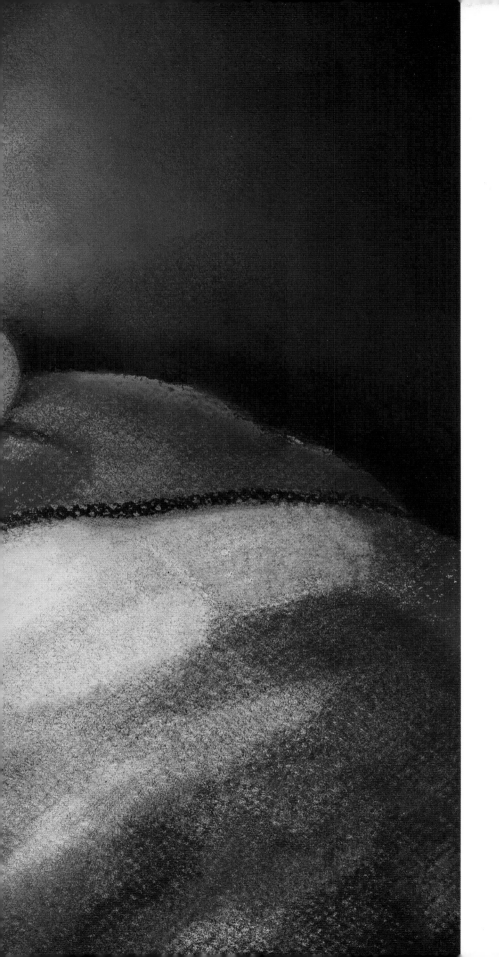

As Robin set off
to find Santa once more,
Little Bear climbed
into bed.

For everyone knows,
that for Santa to come,
little bears really must...

go

to

sleep.

Shhh...

Robin helped Santa search the whole wood —
what gift could he give Little Bear?
A beautiful feather? A sparkly stone? Then...whoosh...up above flew a bright shooting star,

filling the dark sky with light.

The beautiful star swept the sky and shimmered in the snow
where it landed in their path. 'My goodness!' cried Santa.
'*The Magic Christmas Star*! It makes all Christmas wishes come true!'

Robin *just knew* that this would be the *perfect* Christmas present for Little Bear.
So Santa carefully wrapped it up, then hurried off to deliver it...

Three pretty gifts were left under the tree — one for Mum, one for Dad and an extra special one for Little Bear!

His work now done, Santa just
had time for a tasty treat.
Then, with a sprinkle of soft magic dust,
he felt his toes start to tingle.
He dashed to the chimney and
whoosh – he had gone!

But, oops – look what Santa
left behind!

Robin was the first to wake early on Christmas morning.

In fact, he'd hardly slept at all — the night had been too exciting!

Still thinking of the magic star, he flew to see his friend.

Hearing tiny tapping at the window, Little Bear leapt brightly out of the bed.

It was Christmas Day! It had come at last! But had Santa found his way through

all that snow?

Yes, Santa *had* been!
For, *look* — there it was —
the best sooty footprint trail *ever*!
It led past a plate sprinkled
with crumbs, then up to the tree
and the presents!

But one of the boxes tucked
underneath seemed to glow
more brightly than the others.
Carefully, Little Bear untied its bow
...and out burst a magical light!

Little Bear smiled at the Magic Christmas Star and the pretty star smiled right back!

And they both knew, that from then on, they were sure to be...

...forever friends...

A ribbon of stardust trailed behind as the pretty star danced from its box.

Then it sat at the top of the Christmas tree, filling Bear Cottage with magic.

Eyes tightly shut, Little Bear made a wish – for this to be the *best Christmas ever!*

And do you know...

...it was!